Junior Great Books

3

BOOK TWO

Junior Great Books®

3

Gratitude
Courage
Cleverness

BOOK TWO

The Great Books Foundation
A nonprofit educational organization

Published and distributed by

THE GREAT BOOKS FOUNDATION

A nonprofit educational organization

35 East Wacker Drive, Suite 400

Chicago, IL 60601

www.greatbooks.org

CONTENTS

Gratitude

Courage

Cleverness

INTRODUCTION

Welcome to Book Two of Junior Great Books!
Here are some reminders about what to expect as
you use **Shared Inquiry**™—a way of reading and
discussing great stories to explore what they mean.

How Shared Inquiry Works

You will begin by reading along as the story is read aloud. The group then shares questions about the story. Some questions will be answered right away, while others will be saved for the discussion or other activities.

After sharing questions, everyone reads the story again. During the second reading, you will do activities that help you think more deeply about specific parts of the story.

You will then develop your ideas about the story even more in **Shared Inquiry discussion**.

What Shared Inquiry Discussion Looks Like

Your teacher will start the discussion with an **interpretive question**—a question that has more than one good answer that can be supported with evidence from the story. In Shared Inquiry discussion, the goal is not to find the "right answer," but to work together to explore many different answers. Your teacher will ask more questions during the discussion to help everyone think deeply and explain their ideas.

In the discussion, you will give your answer to the interpretive question and back it up with evidence from the story. You will also tell your classmates what you think about their answers and ask them questions to learn more about their ideas.

Depending on the ideas you hear, you may add to or change your original answer to the question. When the discussion is over, people will have different answers to the interpretive question, but everyone will have evidence for those answers and will understand the story better.

Sometimes the class may work on projects after discussion that are related to the story, like writing, making art, or doing research.

You may find that even after the class has finished working on a story, you are still thinking about it. The characters and events in a story may help you think about your own life and the world around you in new ways, or they might bring up a subject you are interested in.

Every time you practice Shared Inquiry activities like asking questions, rereading, and discussing stories, you become a stronger reader and thinker.

Dos and Don'ts in Discussion

DO

Let other people talk, and listen to what they say.

DON'T

Talk while other people are talking.

DO

Share your ideas about the story. You may have an idea no one else has thought of.

DON'T

Be afraid to say what you're thinking about the story.

DO

Be polite when
you disagree
with someone.

DON'T

Get angry when
someone disagrees
with you.

DO

Pay attention to
the person who
is talking.

DON'T

Do things that make
it hard for people
to pay attention.

Shared Inquiry Discussion Guidelines

Following these guidelines in Shared Inquiry discussion will help everyone share ideas about the story and learn from one another.

1 Listen to or read the story twice before the discussion.

2 Discuss only the story that everyone has read.

3 Support your ideas with evidence from the story.

4 Listen to other people's ideas. You may agree or disagree with someone's answer, or ask a question about it.

5 Expect the teacher to only ask questions.

Asking Follow-Up Questions

In Junior Great Books, the teacher isn't the only person who can ask questions. *You* can also ask questions if a classmate says something you want to know more about or understand better. These kinds of questions are called **follow-up questions**.

To ask good follow-up questions, you need to really **listen to what your classmates are saying**. When you listen closely, you hear details that you may want to hear more about. On the next page are some examples of questions you might ask during a discussion or other Junior Great Books activities.

Remember:

- **You can also agree and disagree with your classmates.** Speak directly to them instead of only talking to the teacher, and explain why you agree or disagree.

- **A follow-up question is a compliment.** When you ask a follow-up question, you show that you are listening to and thinking about what others are saying. When someone asks you a question, they are interested in your ideas.

Things you might hear from your classmates:

Follow-up questions you might ask:

Words or phrases that you don't quite understand

"What do you mean?"

"Can you say that again?"

An idea you want to know more about

"Can you say more about that?"

"Why do you think that?"

An idea that needs to be backed up with evidence from the story

"What part of the story made you think that?"

"Where does that happen in the story?"

Theme Introduction

Gratitude

In this section of the book, you will read about characters who both give and receive thanks. Thinking about these stories, and about your own experiences, will give you new ideas about what it means to be grateful.

Important Questions to Think About

Before starting this section, think about your own experiences with gratitude:

- What are some ways that you have shown others that you are grateful?

- Can you think of a time when someone showed gratitude for something you did?

Once you have thought about your own experiences with gratitude, think about this **theme question** and write down your answers or share them aloud:

Should people expect gratitude for doing something kind?

After reading each story in this section, ask yourself the theme question again. You may have some new ideas you want to add.

He knew she was a moon goddess.

WHITE WAVE

Chinese folktale
as told by Diane Wolkstein

In the hills of southern China, there once stood
a shrine. It was made of stones—beautiful
white, pink, and gray stones—and was built as
a house for a goddess.

Now the stones lie scattered on the hillside.
If you should happen to find one, remember
this story . . . of the stones, the shrine, and the
goddess White Wave.

Long ago, in the time of mysteries, a young
farmer was walking home from the fields in
the evening. He walked slowly, for he was not
eager to return to his house. He lived alone.

His parents had died two years before. He was too poor to marry and too shy to speak with any of the young women in his village.

As he passed through a small forest, he saw a stone, a beautiful white stone, gleaming in the moonlight.

The young man, whose name was Kuo Ming, bent over to look at the stone. It wasn't white. It was every color in the rainbow. And when he held it in his hands, he saw it wasn't a stone at all but a snail, a moon snail. And what was the most wonderful good fortune—it was alive!

The farmer gently carried the snail home and placed it in an earthenware jar. Then, before fixing his own dinner, he went out again and gathered fresh leaves for the snail.

The first thing he did the next morning was to look in the jar. The leaves were gone. The snail had eaten

them. Kuo Ming picked four more leaves and went off to the fields to work.

When he came home that evening, the farmer found his dinner waiting for him on the table—a bowl of cooked rice, steamed vegetables, and a cup of hot tea.

He looked around the room. No one was there. He went to the door and looked out into the night. No one. He left the door open, hoping that whoever had prepared his dinner might join him.

The next evening his dinner was again waiting for him—and this time there was a branch of wild peach set in a vase on the table. The farmer made a special trip to the village to ask if strangers had arrived. No one knew of any.

Every morning he left leaves for the snail.
Every evening his dinner was waiting, and
always there was a wildflower in the vase.

One morning Kuo Ming woke up earlier
than usual. He took his rake and started off
as if he were going to the fields. Instead he
circled back to his house and stood outside the
window, listening. There was no sound. Then,
as the first light of the day touched the earth,
he heard a noise.

He looked in the window and saw a tiny
white hand rising from the jar. It rose higher
and higher. Then a second white hand rose
from the jar, and out leaped a beautiful girl.

She was pure light. Her dress was made
of silk, and as she moved her dress rippled,
changing from silver to white to gold.
Wherever she stepped in the room, the
room shone.

He knew, though no one had told him,
that she was a moon goddess. And he knew,
though no one had told him, that he must
never try to touch her.

The next morning, before he went to work,
he watched her, and the next morning, and
the next.

As the days went by, his loneliness
disappeared. He skipped to the fields in the
morning and walked quickly home in the
evening. His dinner was always waiting. The
house was shining. The air was sweet. And his
heart was full.

Many days passed. Then, one morning,
as he was watching her sweep the floor, her
long black hair fell across her face and a great
longing came upon him. He wanted to touch
her hair. The desire burst upon him so strongly
and quickly that he forgot what he knew. He
opened the door and rushed into the room.

"Do not move," she said.

"Who are you?" he asked.

"I am White Wave, the moon goddess. But now I must leave you, for you have forgotten what you knew."

"No!" he cried.

"Good farmer," she said, "if you can hold yourself still and count for me, I will leave you a gift. Let me hear you count. Count to five."

"One," he whispered.

She crossed in front of him and walked toward the open door.

"Two," he said softly.

"I leave you my shell."

"Three," he said more strongly.

"If ever you
are in great need,
call me by my name,
White Wave, and I will
come to you."

"Four," he cried.

There was a streak of
lightning and a great roll of
thunder.

"Five!"

A huge wind came and swept
the goddess into the air. He ran
outside, but the rain poured down
so fast that he could not see her.

He stood in the pouring rain a long
time. Then he went back into the house.
The snail shell was there. He picked it up.
No living creature was inside.

Kuo Ming went to the fields, but he did not
think of his work. He thought only of White
Wave and how to bring her back.

As he was wandering over the hills, his foot
struck a stone. He bent over to look at it. At that
moment, he decided he would build a shrine
for White Wave—a beautiful stone house where

she might live peacefully. He spent more time choosing the stones—beautiful white, pink, and gray stones—than working in the fields. When the harvest came, it was very small. He ate the little there was. He ate the supplies he had stored, and after that he lived on berries and wild grass.

At last, one evening, the shrine was complete. But that evening the farmer was so weak with hunger, he could barely walk. He stumbled into his house and tripped over the earthenware jar. The shell fell out.

Quickly he picked it up, and as he held it, he remembered the words of the goddess: "If ever you are in great need, call me by my name, White Wave . . ."

The farmer held the shell in front of him. Then he raised it in the air, and with his last strength he cried: *White Wave, I need you.*

Slowly he turned the shell toward him. A wave of gleaming white rice cascaded out of the shell and onto the floor. He dipped his hands into it. The rice was solid and firm. It was enough to last him until the next harvest.

He never called her name again. With the flowing of the rice, a new strength had come to him. Kuo Ming worked hard in the fields. The rice grew. The vegetables flourished. He married and had children. But he did not forget White Wave.

He told his wife about her, and when his children were old enough, he took them on his knee and told them the story of White Wave. The children liked to hold the shell in their hands as they listened to the story.

The shrine stood on the hill above their house. The children often went there in the early morning and evening, hoping to see White Wave. They never did.

When the old man died, the shell was lost. In time the shrine, too, disappeared. All that remained was the story.

But that is how it is with all of us: when we die, all that remains is the story.

· *To Luba's astonishment, the little bird spoke.* ·

LUBA AND THE WREN

Ukrainian folktale as told by Patricia Polacco

Once there was a poor farmer and his wife. They lived with their only child, Luba, in a humble dacha in a clearing on the edge of a deep forest.

Their house was crowded and small. The roof leaked. The fences needed mending. The fields, although lovingly tended, were meager and bare. They had little comfort. But their daughter, Luba, was full of joy and free from care as all children should be.

One day, as Luba was looking for mushrooms deep in the forest, she heard a small pitiful cry coming from the tree above her. There she saw the most beautiful, delicate

little wren caught in a fowler's net. She took
pity on this little creature and climbed the
tree to free it. It took wing and sang a glorious
song, then it fluttered down from the sky and
landed on a branch next to her. To Luba's
astonishment, the little bird spoke.

"My dear, how can I ever repay you for
saving my life?" it asked.

When Luba found her voice, she replied.
"I would have done the same for any creature,
little one."

"For your kindness," the bird said, "I shall
grant you any wish that you may ask of me, for
I am enchanted."

"But I am content, I have no wish," Luba said
as she shyly laughed.

"If ever you want for
anything, come to the forest
and call me," the bird said.

Luba ran all the way home
and burst into the house and told
her mother and father about the
enchanted wren.

"Foolish girl!" her mother groaned. "Why
didn't you ask the wren for a bigger house!"

"You know how hard life is for us. . . . We are so poor!" her father said.

"Couldn't you go back and ask?" her mother said wearily.

"Go back to the forest and ask the wren for a bigger house on fertile land," they both pleaded.

Luba did as they asked and went to the edge of the forest.

"Little wren, little wren . . . please come to me," she sang out.

"Dear one," the wren chirped as she landed on a tree branch above Luba, "what is it you wish?"

"It is not mine," Luba said shyly. "It is my parents' wish that brings me back to you."

27

"What, then, do they want?" the wren asked cheerfully.

"A bigger house! They would like to have more room and also to have land that is rich and fertile so they don't have to work so hard to grow things."

"Go then, dear one," the wren said. "For it is already done!"

Sure enough, as Luba got to the clearing where her small dacha had been, there stood a grand farmhouse indeed. Her parents greeted her. Their clothes were new and not patched. Their land was lush and fertile. The orchards were full of trees heavy with ripe fruit.

Luba's heart sang. She knew that her parents would be happy and content.

But, alas, within weeks they were pacing the floor.

"We have been thinking," they said as they paced, "we would like to

have a bigger house, with more fields and workers to help us farm!"

"But I have already asked the wren for this wonderful farm. How can I ask her for more?" said Luba.

"You saved her life," her father said sternly. "She owes this wish to you!"

"Now go and ask the wren for a manor house with acres and acres of land!" her mother ordered.

Luba went to the edge of the forest. She was reluctant to call the little wren, but the wren came as soon as she heard Luba's voice.

"Dear one, what is it now?" the wren asked.

"It is not for me, and I wouldn't ask again, but it is my parents. They no longer like the farmhouse. Now they want an estate with acres of land, and servants."

The wren could see that the child was ashamed.

"Go then, my dear," the wren said. "For it is already done!"

When Luba returned home, there, instead of a big farmhouse, stood a graceful house of estate surrounded by lush gardens, ponds and honking geese, and swans.

As she entered the house, her father was seated by the fireplace in a grand chair. He was truly Lord of the Manor. Her mother was seated next to him, being tended by handmaidens. Spread before them was a great table glowing with all kinds of wondrous things to eat. Now Luba was sure they would be happy and content.

But just as before, Luba awoke one morning to see her parents pacing the floor. "We have been thinking," they began. "Since the wren can grant us anything we want, why didn't we ask for a palace in the first place?"

"But Mama, Papa," Luba pleaded, "I cannot ask the wren again!"

"Ah, but you can!" the father hissed. "After all, you saved her life, didn't you?"

"She should be grateful!" her mother bellowed.

"Go now!" they ordered. "And not only do we want a palace, but we wish to be rulers of all the Ukraine!"

Luba walked slowly to the edge of the forest. Her heart was heavy. The sky was gray and dark. The forest looked bleak and unfriendly. Luba called for the wren. The wren came.

"What is it they wish now?" the wren asked sternly.

"Now they want to live in a palace and be rulers of all the Ukraine!" Luba answered, barely able to speak.

"Go then, my child," the wren said. "It is already done!"

When Luba arrived home, she stood in the courtyard of a majestic palace. Everywhere she looked there were uniformed servants and guards. When she entered the palace, there were her parents, surrounded by chancellors and vice chancellors and noblemen from all the counties and estates in the Ukraine.

I hope that this makes them happy at last! Luba thought.

And they were, for a time. But then one morning Luba awoke to find her parents standing near her bed.

"We have been thinking," they said. "Being rulers of the Ukraine is not what we thought it would be. Go to the wren and ask her to make us the Tzar and Tzarina of all the Russias!"

"This I cannot do!" Luba cried.

"You must!" they said. "After all, we are the rulers of the Ukraine, and you must not disobey!"

When Luba got to the forest, the wren was waiting for her! The sky was full of billowing clouds, gray and stormy. Lightning crackled at their edges.

"Now what do they want?" the wren asked impatiently.

"They want to be the Tzar and Tzarina of all the Russias," Luba answered as she sobbed.

"Go then, it is already done!" the wren sighed.

As Luba approached the clearing, she saw the onion domes of the Tzars gleaming in the sun. Then she saw her parents, the Tzar and Tzarina of all the Russias, drive up in a golden coach, festooned with riches and splendor that she had never imagined in her life.

Surely, she thought to herself, this will finally make them happy and content.

This time it seemed that, at long last, they finally were. Then one day Luba found them pacing the Great Hall. As Luba approached them, they said, "Ah, Luba . . . we were thinking, now that we are Tzar and Tzarina of all the Russias, we see absolutely no reason why we cannot be Emperor and Empress of the entire world!"

Luba could not speak.

"Go to the wren and make this so, we command you!" they growled.

Luba hardly recognized her parents anymore. But she did as they asked.

When she entered the forest this day, the sky was blacker than black. The trees twisted harshly. Storm clouds rolled angrily in the sky. The wind seemed to push against her every step. The wren was waiting for her.

"What now?" the wren snapped.

Luba did not speak for the longest time, but finally she found the words.

"They wish to be Emperor and Empress of all the world!"

"Go then," the wren said. "It is already done."

Luba stood in the majestic throne room. There, seated on the tallest thrones, were her parents, Emperor and Empress of all the world! They didn't even speak to her. Leaders from all lands near and far were bowing at their feet.

At long last! Luba thought. They are happy and content.

Then, one day, as all the times before, she saw her parents standing, looking out of the window of her room.

"We have been thinking," they hissed.
"We want more . . . much, much, much more!
We want to be as gods!"

Luba was stunned. "No Papa . . . Mama! Do
you hear what you are saying? This is sacrilege!"

"Silence!" they thundered. "Go ask the wren!"

Luba went to the forest. Never had the journey taken so long. A fierce storm raged in the sky above her. The wind howled, the trees writhed and shook. But the wren was waiting. Luba could not find the words to ask this wish! She just stood and cried.

"And now?" the wren asked almost sadly.

"They . . . want to be as . . . gods!" Luba choked through her tears.

Lightning slashed the sky in half. The thunder cried out Luba's name; the ground pitched and buckled under her feet.

"Go then, my child," the wren said softly. "It is already done!"

Luba walked sadly back to the clearing.
Her steps were heavy, her heart ached. But as
she reached the clearing . . .

She was astonished to see her little dacha!
That dear little house just as it was before. The
fences needed mending; the roof leaked; the
fields were meager and bare.

Then she saw her mama and papa sitting on
the front porch. Her mother was mending torn
clothing. Her father was carving a small piece
of wood.

"Here is our dear treasure now!" her mother
exclaimed.

"I made this today just for you," her father
said as he showed her a carving of a small
wooden bird.

"Was it wonderful in the forest today?" they
said as they stretched out their arms to her.

Luba leaped into their warm embrace.

At long last, her parents
were happy, and very, very
content indeed.

Basho agreed to share cherries with the foxes.

BASHO AND THE RIVER STONES

Tim Myers

Illustrations by Oki Han

Matsuo Basho is Japan's most famous poet. But few people know how he came to be a lifelong friend to the foxes of Fukagawa.

When he first came to live near the Fuka River, Basho discovered a cherry tree on his property and agreed to share its cherries with the local foxes.

For a long time things were peaceful; between Basho and the fox clan there was great *wa,* or harmony.

But then some of the clan grew impatient and greedy. And one young fox, particularly fond of cherries, decided to play a trick on the poet.

Japanese foxes have great magic; they're especially good at transforming things—and themselves. So the young fox made himself look like a *yamabushi*, a wandering monk . . . and picked three stones out of the river. These he turned into gold coins.

The fox knew Basho was poor. So when he approached the poet's bare little hut and saw Basho reading in the sunshine, he said, in his best monk voice, "A good-hearted merchant gave me these coins, and I want to do a kindness with them in return. I've noticed that the foxes around here look very hungry. If I give you these coins, will you sign a paper saying you'll leave the cherries of that beautiful tree only for them?"

Basho was quite hungry himself. He had little money for food since he spent his time writing and wandering in the woods and fields. And cherries, though delicious, only come once a year. So he agreed, setting the coins carefully on a low table in his hut. Then he picked up his calligraphy brush and wrote what the fox-monk had suggested, signing it with his name. At that the monk went on his way, chuckling to himself.

The next day the young fox couldn't wait to sneak up to the hut; he wanted to see how angry Basho would be once the magic wore off and the coins turned back into stones.

But when he peeked in at the window, he saw Basho writing, with a huge smile on his face and the three river stones on the table before him. The fox was confused. Suddenly Basho noticed the fox's ears sticking up above the window ledge.

"Ah, *kitsune*!" Basho called happily, "come see what good fortune I've had!" The curious fox trotted around the hut and came in through the door.

"Yesterday a monk visited me," Basho began, "and paid me three gold coins to leave all the cherries for you foxes. But some fox must have tricked that monk—because they weren't really coins at all. This morning they turned back into river stones. But see how beautiful they are!" The poet held up one of the water-rounded stones, admiring its smooth surface and rich color.

"At first I was angry and disappointed to lose the gold," Basho continued. "How foolish that was! Suddenly, as I looked carefully at the stones, I understood—and a poem came to me!"

How many years have
these stones loved the river, not
knowing they were poor?

When he heard this, the young fox was amazed. And suddenly he felt ashamed.

"Master!" the fox said sorrowfully, "forgive me! I'm the one who tricked you, pretending to be a monk. I was blind and selfish—but you understood what was really important! I should have remembered that many things are more valuable than gold!"

45

Basho looked surprised, but then he nodded. "A good poem is worth more than money—and it lasts much longer," he said. "Thank you for being honest with me, *kitsune*."

"And thank you for teaching me," the fox said. Then he bowed low and left.

The fox returned to his lair with a heavy heart. Sitting alone, he wondered how he could ever repay the debt of gratitude he now owed Basho.

Then it came to him—the three *riyo* he'd buried beneath the stone lantern at the temple of Inari! Those gold coins—real ones—could buy the poet enough food for the whole winter. The fox dug them up and returned to Basho's hut.

"Master," he said seriously, "you must let me tear up that paper you signed, giving us foxes all the cherries. I was dishonest with you; it shouldn't count!"

But Basho wouldn't hear of it, as the fox had expected. "I'm afraid I can't let you do that," Basho said. "I accept your kind apology, but I've already signed the paper. It would be dishonorable to pretend I hadn't."

"Then at least let me pay you for the cherries!" the fox pleaded, showing Basho the coins and assuring him they were real.

"Ah, *kitsune*—I don't mean to be difficult. But you already paid me for the cherries. The river stones you gave were beautiful, and they helped me find a poem; that was more than enough! My honor won't allow me to accept charity."

Again the fox left feeling guilty and perplexed.

Slowly he made his way through the woods to the banks of the Fuka River, pausing there with his head hung in shame. But he happened to glance at the purling water and noticed, just beneath its surface, more beautiful river stones. Suddenly he lifted his head and smiled. *Now I know what to do!* he told himself.

The next day he returned to Basho's hut, carrying a small bag. Basho frowned when he saw the fox approaching. Would the creature try to give him the coins again?

"Master," the fox said, bowing deeply, "I thought about what you said—and I understand. So today I've come, not with charity, but with a small gift to show my appreciation." At that the fox turned the little bag upside down.

Out tumbled three beautiful river stones.

Basho's face broke into a glowing smile. "Ah, *kitsune!*" he said. "What a perfect gift! Yes, I accept them— perhaps they'll inspire another poem. Thank you. You are too kind!"

The fox could hardly contain his happiness; but then he said, hesitating a little, "So . . . you promise to keep my gift?"

"Of course," Basho answered, reaching down to stroke the fox's head.

"Oh, Master!" the fox exclaimed, "I am so pleased!" With that he scampered off.

That night, before Basho went to his sleeping mat, he looked at the three new stones where he'd set them on his table. Then he smiled to himself and blew out the candle.

When he woke with the sun the next morning, he sat up and stretched—but suddenly stopped. For there on the table—just where he'd left the river stones—were three gold coins, glinting in the light from the window!

Basho hurriedly went to the table, picking up each of the coins and feeling it. They were real—he was sure of it.

Looking closer, he realized they were the same coins the fox had tried to give him before!

Suddenly he understood—and burst out laughing. They hadn't been river stones at all! The magical fox had tricked him again!

What a clever kitsune! the poet said to himself—*for he knows I must keep a promise— even one he tricked me into making.* So Basho picked up the coins and said a quick prayer of gratitude, knowing he could now buy food for the winter.

Thinking the fox might be watching from somewhere, he went to the door and stepped outside to call him in. But all he saw was a paper fastened to the wall of the hut.

Dear Master:

Thank you again for promising to keep the gift! And just as the first river stones inspired you to write a haiku, these have inspired me . . .

I've eaten cherries alone—
but they're much sweeter
when shared with a friend.

Ah, kitsune! thought Basho.

So from that day on, Basho and the foxes shared the cherries as before—and many other things.

Theme Introduction

Courage

In this section of the book, you will read about characters who find and show courage in different ways. Thinking about these stories, and about your own experiences, will give you new ideas about what it means to have courage.

Important Questions to Think About

Before starting this section, think about your own experiences with courage:

- Can you think of a time when you struggled to have courage?

- How do you find courage when you have to do something that scares you?

Once you have thought about your own experiences with courage, think about this **theme question** and write down your answers or share them aloud:

How does a person gain courage?

After reading each story in this section, ask yourself the theme question again. You may have some new ideas you want to add.

He heard a voice crying out from the shadows.

THE MONSTER
WHO GREW SMALL

Joan Grant

Far to the South, beyond the Third Cataract,
there was a small village where a certain boy
lived with his uncle. The uncle was known as
the Brave One because he was a hunter and
killed such a lot of large animals, and he was
very horrid to his nephew because he thought
the boy was a coward. He tried to frighten him
by telling stories of the terrible monsters that
he said lived in the forest, and the boy believed
what he was told, for was not his uncle called
the Brave One, the Mighty Hunter?

Whenever the boy had to go down to the river he thought that crocodiles would eat him, and when he went into the forest he thought that the shadows concealed snakes and that hairy spiders waited under the leaves to pounce on him. The place that always felt especially dangerous was on the path down to the village, and whenever he had to go along it he used to run.

One day, when he came to the most frightening part of this path, he heard a voice crying out from the shadows of the darkest trees. He put his fingers in his ears and ran even faster, but he could still hear the voice. His fear was very loud, but even so he could hear his heart, and it said to him:

"Perhaps the owner of that voice is much more frightened than you are. You know what it feels like to be frightened. Don't you think you ought to help?"

So he took his fingers out of his ears, and clenched his fists to make himself feel braver, and plunged into the deep shade, thrusting

his way between
thorn trees in the
direction of the cries.

He found a Hare caught by the
leg in a tangle of creepers, and the Hare said
to him, "I was so very frightened, but now you
have come I am not afraid anymore. You must
be very brave to come alone into the forest."

The boy released the Hare and quieted it
between his hands, saying, "I am not at all
brave. In my village they call me Miobi, the
Frightened One. I should never have dared to
come here, only I heard you calling."

The Hare said to him, "Why are you
frightened? What are you frightened of?"

"I am frightened of the crocodiles who live
in the river and of the snakes and the spiders
that lie in wait for me whenever I go out. But
most of all I am frightened of the Things which
rustle in the palm thatch over my bed place—
my uncle says they are only rats and lizards,
but *I* know they are far worse than that."

"What you want," said the Hare, "is a house
with walls three cubits thick, where you could
shut yourself away from all the things you fear."

"I don't think that would do any good,"
said Miobi. "For if there were no windows I
should be afraid of not being able to breathe,
and if there *were* windows I should always be

watching them, waiting for Things to creep in
to devour me."

The Hare seemed to have stopped being
frightened, and Miobi said to it, "Now that you
know that I am not at all brave, I don't suppose
I'll seem much of a protection. But if you feel
I'd be better than nothing I'll carry you home,
if you'll tell me where you live."

To Miobi's astonishment, the Hare replied,
"I live in the Moon, so you can't come home
with me, yet. But I should like to give you
something to show how grateful I am for your
kindness. What would you like to have best in
the world?"

"I should like to have Courage . . . but I
suppose that's one of the things which can't
be given."

"I can't *give* it to you, but I can tell you
where to find it. The road that leads there you
will have to follow alone. But when your fears
are strongest, look up to the Moon and I will
tell you how to overcome them."

Then the Hare told Miobi about the road
he must follow, and the next morning, before
his uncle was awake, the boy set out on his

journey. His only weapon was a dagger that
the Hare had given him. It was long and keen,
pale as moonlight.

Soon the road came to a wide river. Then
Miobi was very frightened, for in it there
floated many crocodiles, who watched him
with their evil little eyes. But he remembered
what the Hare had told him, and after looking
up to the Moon, he shouted at them:

"If you want to be killed come and
attack me!"

Then he plunged into the river,
his dagger clutched in his hand,
and began to swim
to the far bank.

60

Much to the crocodiles' surprise, they found themselves afraid of him. To try to keep up their dignity, they said to each other, "He is too thin to be worth the trouble of eating!" And they shut their eyes and pretended not to notice him. So Miobi crossed the river safely and went on his way.

After a few more days he saw two snakes, each so large that it could have swallowed an ox without getting a pain. Both speaking at the same time, they said loudly, "If you come one step further we shall immediately eat you."

Miobi was very frightened, for snakes were one of the things he minded most. He was on the point of running away when he looked up to the Moon, and immediately he knew what the Hare wanted him to do.

"O Large and Intelligent Serpents," he said politely, "a boy so small as myself could do no more than give *one* of you a satisfactory meal. Half of me would not be worth the trouble of digesting. Hadn't you better decide between yourselves by whom I am to have the honor of being eaten?"

"Sensible, very. I will eat you myself," said the first serpent.

"No you won't, he's mine," said the second.

"Nonsense, you had that rich merchant. He was so busy looking after his gold that he never noticed you until you got him by the legs."

"Well, what about the woman who was admiring her face in a mirror? You said she was the tenderest meal you'd had for months."

"The merchant was *since* that," said the first serpent firmly.

"He wasn't."

"He was."

"Wasn't!"

"Was!!"

While the serpents were busy arguing which of them should eat Miobi, he had slipped past without their noticing, and was already out of sight. So that morning neither of the serpents had even a small breakfast.

Miobi felt so cheerful that he began to whistle. For the first time, he found himself enjoying the shapes of trees and the colors of flowers instead of wondering what dangers they might be concealing.

Soon he came in sight of a village, and even in the distance he could hear a sound of lamentation. As he walked down the single street no one took any notice of him, for the people were too busy moaning and wailing. The cooking fires were unlit, and goats were bleating because no one had remembered to milk them. Babies were crying because they were hungry, and a small girl was yelling because she had fallen down and cut her knee and her mother wasn't even interested. Miobi went to the house of the Headman, whom he found sitting cross-legged, with ashes on his head, his eyes shut, and his fingers in his ears.

Miobi had to shout very loud to make him hear. Then the old man opened one ear and one eye and growled, "What do you want?"

"Nothing," said Miobi politely. "I wanted to ask what *you* wanted. Why is your village so unhappy?"

"You'd be unhappy," said the Headman crossly, "if you were going to be eaten by a Monster."

"Who is going to be eaten? You?"

"Me and everyone else, even the goats. Can't you hear them bleating?"

Miobi was too polite to suggest that the goats were only bleating because no one had milked them. So he asked the Headman, "There seems to be quite a lot of people in your village. Couldn't you kill the Monster if you all helped?"

"Impossible!" said the Headman. "Too big, too fierce, too terrible. We are *all* agreed on that."

64

"What does the Monster look like?" asked
Miobi.

"They say it has the head of a crocodile and
the body of a hippopotamus and a tail like a
very fat snake, but it's sure to be even worse.
Don't talk about it!" He put his
hands over his face and
rocked backwards and
forwards, moaning to
himself.

"If you will tell me
where the Monster
lives, I will try to kill it
for you," said Miobi, much to
his own surprise.

"Perhaps you are wise," said the Headman,
"for then you will be eaten first and won't have
so long to think about it. The Monster lives
in the cave on the top of that mountain. The
smoke you can see comes from his fiery breath,
so you'll be cooked before you are eaten."

Miobi looked up to the Moon and he knew
what the Hare wanted him to say, so he said it:

"I will go up to the mountain and challenge
the Monster."

Climbing the mountain took him a long time, but when he was halfway up he could see the Monster quite clearly. Basking at the mouth of its cave, its fiery breath wooshing out of its nostrils, it looked about three times as big as the Royal Barge—which is very big, even for a monster.

Miobi said to himself, "I won't look at it again until I have climbed all the distance between me and the cave. Otherwise I might feel too much like running away to be able to go on climbing."

When next he looked at the Monster he expected it to be much larger than it had seemed from farther away. But instead it looked quite definitely smaller, only a little bigger than one Royal Barge instead of three. The Monster saw him. It snorted angrily, and the snort flared down the mountainside and scorched Miobi. He ran back rather a long way before he could make himself stop. Now the Monster seemed to have grown larger again. It was *quite* three times as large as the Royal Barge—perhaps four.

Miobi said to himself, "This is very curious indeed. The farther I run away from the Monster, the larger it seems, and the nearer I am to it, the smaller it seems. Perhaps if I was *very* close it might be a reasonable size for me to kill with my dagger."

So that he would not be blinded by the fiery breath, he shut his eyes. And so that he would not drop his dagger, he clasped it very tightly. And so that he would not have time to start being frightened, he ran as fast as he could up the mountain to the cave.

When he opened his eyes he couldn't see anything which needed killing. The cave seemed empty, and he began to think that he must have run in the wrong direction. Then he felt something hot touch his right foot. He looked down, and there was the Monster—and it was as small as a frog! He picked it up in his hand and scratched its back. It was no more than comfortably warm to hold, and it made a small, friendly sound, halfway between a purr and the simmer of a cooking pot.

67

Miobi thought, "Poor little Monster! It will feel so lonely in this enormous cave." Then he thought, "It might make a nice pet, and its fiery breath would come in useful for lighting my cooking fire." So he carried it carefully down the mountain, and it curled up in his hand and went to sleep.

When the villagers saw Miobi, at first they thought they must be dreaming, for they had been so sure the Monster would kill him. Then they acclaimed him as a hero, saying, "Honor to the mighty hunter! He, the bravest of all! He, who has slain the Monster!"

Miobi felt very embarrassed, and as soon as he could make himself heard above the cheering, he said, "But I didn't kill it. I brought it home as a pet."

They thought that was only the modesty becoming to a hero, and before they would believe him he had to explain how the Monster had only seemed big so long as he was running away, and that the nearer he got to it the smaller it grew, until at last, when he was standing beside it, he could pick it up in his hand.

The people crowded round to see the Monster. It woke up, yawned a small puff of smoke, and began to purr. A little girl said to Miobi, "What is its name?"

"I don't know," said Miobi, "I never asked it."

It was the Monster himself who answered her question. He stopped purring, looked round to make sure everyone was listening, and then said:

"I have many names. Some call me Famine, and some Pestilence, but the most pitiable of humans give me their own names." It yawned again, and then added, "But most people call me What-Might-Happen."

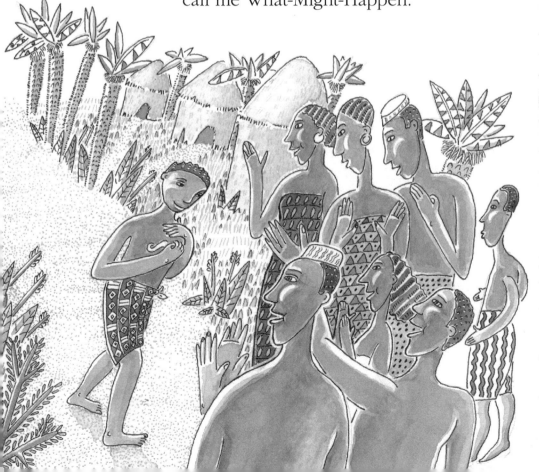

· *Wrap this round you and think of me.* ·

THE BUFFALO STORM

Katherine Applegate

I was not afraid of anything
(except maybe storms).
I'd coaxed a wild-eyed colt to take a saddle,
and climbed the oak by my grandmother's
   barn
higher than all the boys,
cloud-catching high.
I was not afraid of anything,
so when my papa said, We're going west
   to Oregon,
I begged to drive the oxen team
across the endless prairie.

I couldn't say the truth of it,
not until the night before the wagon rolled,
when I helped my grandmother
put the barn to bed one last time—
my grandmother,
who could bake a cake or birth a calf or build
    a barn;
my grandmother,
who did not much like storms, either.
I'm not going to Oregon, I told her.
You need me here to pick the best berries
and name the new kittens
and help make a wish on the first firefly
    of summer.

You need me here when the storms come
  strong
and you are afraid—
when we are afraid, together.

I need you so, my grandmother said,
but your mama and papa need you more,
with the journey ahead and the new baby
  coming.
From her pocket she pulled out paper and
  envelopes,
a sharp-tipped pen, and a jar of night-blue ink.
Write it all down for me, Hallie, she said,
all the things I've heard tell of—
the prairie dogs clowning,
the coyotes making crazy music.
You'll see buffalo,
  child, too many to
  count.
What a gift to hear
  the earth rumble
  as they run!
I ran my fingers
  over paper
cool and smooth.

At dawn, the wagon waited, oiled canvas top
   gleaming
like a bread loaf ready for the oven.
Papa fussed, said forty head of oxen couldn't
   budge this wagon.
Too much is coming.
Too much, I thought, is getting left behind.
Into my arms my grandmother placed
the quilt she'd stitched while still a girl.
When a storm starts, she said,
wrap this round you and think of me.
She hugged me close and her coat smelled
   sharp and sweet,
of hay and horse and pine.
She whispered the words so I would know
   how much they mattered:

I am old and this is home,
but I'll be with you just the same.

We joined other wagons,
like beads slowly stringing.
Papa let me drive the team, though some said
I was too young and green, and a girl, to boot.
At night we circled. Fires spat and crackled,
children danced, babies drowsed.
Men boasted of the buffalo they would shoot
just to watch their great bodies fall.

Mama handed me the pen and the crisp,
   waiting paper.
Which way is home? I asked.
She pointed to my heart. There inside, she said,
there is home.
But I knew inside was just
   a hard place hurting.
I put the pen away.

The first storm came deep in the
   Nebraska night,
spun out of too much quiet.
Hail hurled down,
rain bounced off the stubborn earth.
I hid under my grandmother's quilt,
shaking fingers tracing the careful stitches.
Back home, she'd sing while the thunder
   rolled,

but now her voice was lost to me
as furious lightning split the sky
and the animals bellowed in fear.
I could not even hear myself cry.

The next morning, a creek was waiting to
    be crossed,
swollen with rain and looking for trouble.
Mud sucked at the wheels while
    the oxen groaned.
We hit a rock and the
    wagon lurched,
pitching me into the
    icy water.
The current tried to
    swallow me whole,
but I hung tight to
    a wheel
till Papa hauled me
    in like a fish.

You're a tough one, he said, when you want
    to be—
as long as there's no thunder around.
Mama held me.
We're all of us
afraid of something, she said.

Weeks wove together and faded in the sun.
By the time we reached Wyoming,
the oxen hooves were bleeding
and my toes showed through my shoes.
One day during the nooning,
I searched for buffalo chips to feed the fire.
I rounded a sandstone ridge, and when I
    looked back,
the wagons had vanished in the dusty air.
I'm not afraid, I told a skittering lizard.
I couldn't say the truth of it,
not with the clouds so low and fierce.
A cry cut the stillness, and I spun around,
searching out the sound.

Past the ridge I saw her—
a little buffalo calf, red gold, bawling,
leg wedged in a rocky place.

Her mother stomped and snorted,
riled as the black sky,
tail twirling like a lariat.
The calf cried again, and I knew what I had
   to do.
I was not afraid of anything
(except maybe those angry clouds).
She'd be no more trouble than a wild-eyed colt,
the one I'd tamed with my grandmother's help.

I shinnied down sharp rocks.
The calf blinked at me with eyes like wet
   marbles.
I neared her slowly,
soothing, Whoa, girl, whoa,
her breath wild and warm on my face.

I pushed and yanked and grunted;
she kicked and complained and fretted;
and then, with one last great heave,
she was free.
I watched her run, clumsy and stiff legged,
to her mother's nuzzled scolding.

Suddenly, a noise like boulders breaking
shook the air,
and I knew a storm was coming,
bigger and louder than any I'd known,
a storm like no other.
Dust billowed, a thick brown fog.
I dropped to the dirt and covered my ears,
waiting for lightning to tear the sky,
trembling so hard that the earth itself
began to tremble, too,
and then I remembered my grandmother's
    words—
What a gift to hear the earth rumble as
    they run!
—and I knew.

Across the land the buffalo thundered,
huge and surly and crazed with life.
I stood, I stared,
I yelped with joy at the sight of it.
On and on, for miles and miles,
they moved like a black ocean surging,
an ocean without end.
Fine storm! I shouted,
and laughed just the way I knew
my grandmother would have laughed.
What a gift, I thought,
feeling my grandmother there,
there with me at last.

When finally they were gone,
the calf and her mother loping behind,
the air went silent as a prayer.
Dark clouds knotted in the sky
and blowing sand stung my cheeks,
but I kept walking.
When thunder rumbled, I didn't flinch or hide
    or cry.
It seemed harmless as a puppy's growl,
a tinny echo of something much grander.
At last, the wagons came into view
and then the rains began.

By the time we made Oregon,
my wool dress was worn and patched
as my grandmother's quilt.
The air tasted of autumn,
but the soil was deep and rich and
    waiting.
Hope grows big here, Papa said,
big like the trees.
I helped him make a simple cabin
to see the family through the
    winter.
A palace, Mama said.

I wrote my letter the day my sister was born.
Dear Grandmother, it read,
We named the baby Olympia—
my idea, after you.
When storms come, I will wrap her in your
    quilt
and hold her close,
just the way you used to hold me.
Oregon's a fine place,
with trees just right for climbing.
It's home now for me,
this new, wild place,
but I promise I'll be with you,
just the same.

· *"What a dream!" Pierre exclaimed.* ·

PIERRE'S DREAM

Jennifer Armstrong

Some time ago, in the town of Apt, which is not far from Avignon, there lived a lazy, foolish man named Pierre. He had no job, no interests, and no hobby besides sitting under the olive trees in the afternoon, thinking of dinner.

One day Pierre walked aimlessly through a field, nibbling sunflower seeds and spitting out the husks. In this field was a large tree, and Pierre sat under it to rest. In no time at all he fell asleep and snored loudly enough to startle the crows.

While he slept, the Grand Circus des Étoiles pitched its tents in the field, ranged its painted

wagons around, and strung up a rope corral
for the trick ponies. When Pierre awoke, it was
to find himself in the midst of a bustling village
that had not been there before.

"Aha," he said. "I must be dreaming."

He rose and looked about him. He had a
wonderful sense of accomplishment. All this,
all he surveyed—all was his dream. Pierre was
very pleased with himself.

As he stood admiring the work of his
imagination, a shout of alarm filled the air.

"The lion! He has escaped!"

Dozens of circus folk fled past Pierre, their
colored costumes twinkling in the sunshine.

Then bounding around the corner came a dreadful, snarling lion. His teeth gleamed. His roars made the leaves tremble on the trees. Pierre felt a bit nervous.

"Very realistic," he murmured.

But as it was his dream, or so he thought, he had no fear. "For, of course, I can wake up at any time," he reminded himself.

And so, smiling confidently, Pierre held up one hand.

"Stop, lion!" he commanded. "Back! Go back!"

So strong was Pierre's voice that the lion stopped his charge. He peered around, and then with his tail tucked between his legs the lion turned and slunk back to his cage.

"Well, that's that," Pierre said. "I'm enjoying this dream very much."

"Oh, monsieur! You are so brave!" called out the dainty trapeze artist from high above.

Pierre smiled modestly. "May I join you, mademoiselle?"

"Please do," she replied, twirling her parasol.

Pierre examined the pole to which the high wire was strung. He would never attempt such a thing normally, but as it was his dream, or so he thought, Pierre knew he could climb with no effort at all.

Up he went, hand over hand into the air. At the top he had a magnificent view of the countryside all around.

"Yoo-hoo!" called the dainty trapeze artist from the far end of the wire.

Pierre bowed like a courtier, and stepped boldly onto the high wire. It swayed and dipped under his foot.

"Very realistic," he murmured.

But as it was his dream, or so he thought, he had no fear. Pierre walked without hesitation to the middle of the wire.

A crowd of circus folk stared up from below.

"I'll give them a thrill," Pierre said to himself.

"Ooooh!" the crowd gasped as he stood on one foot.

"Aaaah!" the crowd sighed as he hopped up and clicked his heels together.

"Ooooh!" the crowd moaned as Pierre stood on his hands.

With that Pierre skipped cheerfully to the end of the wire and kissed the trapeze artist's hand. He was enjoying this dream very much.

"Can you also swallow swords?" asked the snake charmer.

"Can you also juggle fire?" asked the bearded lady.

"Can you also lie down beneath the elephant's foot?" asked the son of the red-haired clown.

Pierre answered all these questions with a smile and a nod. "But, of course," he replied. In dreams, he knew, one can do anything.

The circus folk voted to make him their ringmaster, as the owner of the Grand Circus des Étoiles was in bed with a stomachache. Pierre put on the top hat and tailcoat, and stretched out his legs for two small boys to polish the tall black boots.

"It's Pierre!" gasped the crowd when he stepped into the ring.

"Pierre!"

"Pierre!"

Pierre bowed to the audience. They knew
him, of course, for why should not the people
of Apt also be in his dream?

"They all think I am a lazy, foolish man,"
Pierre told himself. "Tonight they shall see they
are wrong."

Pierre cracked his whip. "Send in the
ponies!"

One, two, three, four, five—six pretty ponies
cantered into the ring, tossing their manes and
setting the bells on their headdresses ajingle.
Pierre stood in the center, cracking his whip
and keeping the ponies at a spirited pace.

"What will he do?" the audience wondered aloud.

"What is Pierre up to?"

The dust flew from under the ponies' hooves and tickled Pierre's nose. The wind from their passing fanned his cheeks.

"Very realistic," he murmured.

Then with a victorious cry he leaped onto the back of the nearest pony, and stood up with his arms crossed. The audience cheered.

"Pierre!"

"What a marvel!"

"Superb!"

After riding each trick pony in turn, Pierre sent them galloping out of the ring and ordered in the knife thrower. Then, to the astonishment of the audience, he calmly allowed the one-eyed man to throw seventeen daggers around him.

After this he hung by one foot from the trapeze, while juggling flaming hoops above a cage of tigers and panthers from the East. The

beasts roared horribly, and the flames singed
Pierre's eyebrows. But as it was his dream, or
so he thought, he had no fear.

He went on to perform many other daring
and death-defying feats, and the audience
greeted each new act with wild applause.

"Pierre!"

"What skill and courage!"

"Extraordinary!"

By the end of the evening Pierre had put
on nearly the entire circus single-handedly.
After the last spectator left the tent, the circus
folk lined up and clapped for Pierre as he trod
wearily across the sawdust.

"You must rest," whispered the dainty trapeze artist.

Pierre nodded. He was tired. Never before had a dream lasted so long, nor left him so fatigued.

The sickly ringleader rode in on a goat cart. "The Grand Circus des Étoiles thanks you," he muttered to Pierre.

"It was my pleasure," Pierre replied.

With that he went out and gazed up at the stars in the sky. A long dream, and a very full one, he decided. Then he sat down under a tree, and closed his eyes.

When at last he opened them again, the sun was high in the sky, and the field around him was empty.

"What a dream!" Pierre exclaimed, stretching his arms.

He smiled, and gazed around him contentedly. There was nothing special he wanted to do. There never was. He was truly a lazy, foolish man, with no job, no interests, and no hobby besides sitting under the olive trees in the afternoon, thinking of dinner.

With a yawn Pierre leaned back against the tree, and knocked the black top hat over his eyes.

"What's this?" he asked in astonishment.

He looked wildly around, bewildered and bemused. Next to the tree, on the ground, was a dainty parasol with a slip of paper pinned to the frill.

Pierre picked it up with a trembling hand.

"Au revoir, Pierre," it read.

Slowly, slowly Pierre began to smile. Then he began to laugh. And as he looked up through the leaves of the olive tree, he had much more to think of than just his dinner.

Theme Introduction

Cleverness

In this section of the book, you will read about characters who do and say clever things. Thinking about these stories, and about your own experiences, will give you new ideas about the different ways to be clever.

IMPORTANT QUESTIONS TO THINK ABOUT

Before starting this section, think about your own experiences with cleverness:

- Can you remember a time when you did something funny, tricky, or smart?

- When is it a good thing to be clever? When is it not a good thing?

Once you have thought about your own experiences with being clever, think about this **theme question** and write down your answers or share them aloud:

What does it mean to be clever?

After reading each story in this section, ask yourself the theme question again. You may have some new ideas you want to add.

"I'm going to learn how to weave dreams."

The Dream Weaver

Concha Castroviejo

Rogelia was a good-for-nothing little girl. That was what her sisters and her schoolmistress said.

She was asked questions at school about the day's lesson, and she was so busy daydreaming she didn't know what she was being asked; at home they told her to iron handkerchiefs so that she'd learn how to do the ironing, and she burned them; to fill the coffee cups at meals, and she spilled coffee on the tablecloth; to water the plants, and the water dripped all over the floor.

"This girl is very clumsy," said her sister Camila, who was very capable and quite conceited.

"This girl is stupid," her sister Pepa would add.

"There's no telling whether this girl will learn or not," the schoolmistress sighed.

The worst of it was that Rogelia never learned how to make bobbin lace. Her granny, her sisters, and her aunts—all the women in her house—were very skillful with the bobbins and made beautiful lace with stars, birds, and flowers, fashioning all sorts of whimsical designs with the threads. This pleased Rogelia a great deal. She would sit down beside her granny, with her little sewing cushion full of pins, threads, and bobbins on her knees, and begin to dream of making wonderful designs. But she dreamed of her designs so intently, and planned them in her head so enthusiastically, that the bobbins collided, tangling the threads; the pins fell out of place, undoing the knots; and her handiwork ended up a sorry mess.

Rogelia burst into tears and felt ashamed as her older sisters began reprimanding her.

"Go get the tissue paper ready to wrap up our lacework," Camila would say to her. "That's all you're good for."

And that was how things went for Rogelia every day.

One afternoon she was peering out the window and saw a very old woman pass by the house, gazing at the sky. Rogelia, who was a very well-mannered girl, ran to the door and

went out into the street, because it seemed that
the old woman was about to trip and fall. But
the old woman laughed and said to her, "Don't
worry. I'm looking at the clouds. By doing so,
the work I do later on turns out so nicely."

"What sort of work do you do?" Rogelia asked
her.

The woman answered, "I'm a weaver of
dreams."

Those words excited Rogelia.

"What a fine occupation!" she exclaimed, and
then she asked, "What is your name, señora?"

"My name is Gosvinda."

Rogelia would have liked to follow along after
old Gosvinda, but she did not dare. She remained
at the door watching her, and saw her walk all
the way down the long street, leave the town,
and go into the woods. From that day on, Rogelia
thought only of the dream weaver. At school she
was more and more inattentive; she burned more
and more clothes as she did the ironing, spilled
more and more water as she watered the flower
pots, and made an even worse tangle of the
pins, threads, and bobbins when she sat down
alongside her granny to make lace.

"This girl is going to have to be sent to a boarding school to see if they can manage to teach her something," her sister Pepa said one day.

"A place where they keep her locked up and punish her," her sister Camila added.

"Where they won't allow her to while away her time gazing at clouds," Pepa piped up again.

"She isn't good for anything," her aunt said.

Then Rogelia said to her sisters, "Since I must learn something, I'm going to learn how to weave dreams."

And her sisters laughed at her.

But Rogelia packed two changes of clothes, a jacket, and her rain boots into a cardboard box, put on a bonnet that she kept to wear on feast days, gave her granny a goodbye kiss, and took off on her own.

Rogelia left the town and reached the woods. It was dark there because the tops of the trees were so dense. Rogelia walked on for a long time until at last she came upon an open meadow, and in the meadow was a house with its walls painted pink and its windows green, surrounded on every side with yellow flowers. The house had seven chimneys through which poured out lovely smoke that looked like no other, a different color puffing out from each chimney.

Rogelia pushed on the door, which was unlocked, and went into the house. From the kitchen, she climbed up to a bedroom, and from the bedroom, she climbed up to the loft, and from the loft, she saw the clouds and mountains in the distance. Old Gosvinda worked there in the loft all day, weaving one dream after another. The smoke of the dreams was what was escaping by way of the chimneys.

On reaching the loft, Rogelia said, "Good day, Señora Gosvinda."

The weaver was not surprised to see the little girl.

"I knew you'd come," she said, answering her greeting.

Rogelia looked all around. She saw the
distaffs and the looms with threads of crystal,
gold, and silver, with threads the color of
emeralds and sapphires. In one corner there
were twelve mice grooming their whiskers.

"I've come to stay, if you'll allow me to," she
said to Gosvinda. "I wish to learn to weave
dreams. At home they tell me I'm useless, but
it may be that I'm suited for such a wonderful
occupation."

Gosvinda replied that she could stay and
explained to her that she needed a girl to help
her because she had a great many orders to fill.
People kept needing more and more dreams.

Rogelia remained in the house in the woods.
Very early each morning, she went up to the

loft and learned to thread the looms and ready the tufts to be spun into threads on the distaff. The threads glided in and out until they formed the weft under the old weaver's hand, and the distaff spun faster and faster, raising a breeze that made the mice sneeze. During the day the cuckoos, and at nightfall the swifts, came and went through the window, bringing in their beaks the orders sent by princes from their royal palaces and by miners from the depths of their caves. All the men and women who knew the weaver ordered dreams from her.

"Once upon a time there used to be seven of us weavers," Gosvinda said to Rogelia, "but my companions retired to take their rest and left me by myself. They were older than I. When I grow weary and retire, there will be no one left at all."

"And what will people do then?" Rogelia asked.

"They'll manufacture pills so they can have synthetic dreams. And children will weave their own dreams for themselves."

Little by little, Rogelia learned to make lovely woven fabrics of the color and shape of clouds. She learned how to make the rainbow tarry by singing to it, and how to wrap it up in orange-colored dreams. She learned to weave pink and blue dreams for the young, and green ones to console those who were sick and those who were sad. And white dreams so that children could embroider them in color.

"You're a very clever little girl," old Gosvinda told her.

And that made Rogelia feel very happy.

"Oh, my!" she replied. "If only those back home could see me!"

"They would still find you useless. If you say you weave dreams, people will laugh at you."

Dreams, once they were woven, came out of the chimneys in a lacework of smoke, and the wind blew them to distant houses. Rogelia soon learned to sweep the floor and to put pots on the fire. Every week a bear brought old Gosvinda wood, rabbits took care of supplying her with vegetables, and blackbirds arrived with fruit.

"What a beautiful house!" Rogelia sighed.

Rogelia learned the weaver's craft so well that dreams now held no secrets for her. Because she worked with them so much with her hands, they no longer lodged in her head. She paid careful attention to the thin, fragile threads, to the delicate interweaving formed by the branches of the trees and the patterns made by the clouds, and to the colors of the rainbow that appeared above the sharp-pointed roof of the little house. Rogelia's mind was never in a daze now, for the dreams were no longer in her head, but in her hands. "When I want a dream for myself," she thought, "I shall weave the most beautiful one that has ever existed."

One day old Gosvinda said to her, "In order to find out if this is your true calling, you must put it to the test: return home and work there."

Rogelia realized that she was obliged to obey.
She went to her cardboard box and put on a
dress that she had woven with the leftovers
from the distaff tufts and that gleamed with the
colors of flowers.

Rogelia returned home, greeted everyone, and
said that she had been learning to be capable.
In the beginning her sisters laughed at her, but
Rogelia's hands were blessed. If she sat down
to make bobbin lace, the bobbins crossed back
and forth like castanets and the threads turned
into lace, with birds, flowers, and clouds in
the white background that looked like a snow-

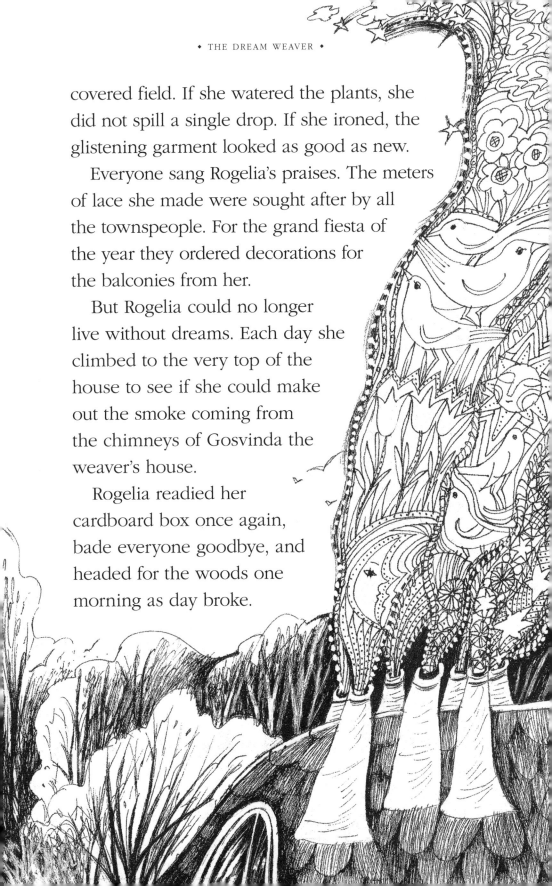

covered field. If she watered the plants, she did not spill a single drop. If she ironed, the glistening garment looked as good as new.

Everyone sang Rogelia's praises. The meters of lace she made were sought after by all the townspeople. For the grand fiesta of the year they ordered decorations for the balconies from her.

But Rogelia could no longer live without dreams. Each day she climbed to the very top of the house to see if she could make out the smoke coming from the chimneys of Gosvinda the weaver's house.

Rogelia readied her cardboard box once again, bade everyone goodbye, and headed for the woods one morning as day broke.

"Good day!" she said as she entered the loft.

The weaver was seated in her corner, and the mice were holding in place the tufts that she was putting on the distaffs.

"I knew you would come," she said, answering Rogelia's greeting. "Now you will stay here forevermore."

Rogelia remained with old Gosvinda. She welcomed the cuckoos and the swifts, fed the mice, helped the bear unload the wood, and placed the vegetables and fruit that the rabbits and the blackbirds brought into their proper baskets. But above all, she kept weaving and weaving. She wove the most complicated and difficult dreams, the ones that tired old Gosvinda. She attended to everything, for she had so many dreams in her hands that none were left in her head. She was so fond of her dreams and so proud of her work that she never dared to keep them.

Each year she went to the town to visit her grandmother, her sisters, and her aunt. She greeted them and then went off once again.

One day a very serious looking gentleman, carrying a large briefcase full of registers with black oilcloth covers, came knocking at the door of Gosvinda's house. Rogelia came down from the loft to see what he wanted, and the gentleman told her that he had come to find out who lived there and what their occupation was so he could write their names down in the tax registers.

"Old Gosvinda and I live here," Rogelia explained to him, "and we are weavers of dreams."

The gentleman looked through his registers and said that such an occupation was not on any list. Then he cleared his throat and left.

"Is it possible that someone is trickier than I?"

THE MAN WHOSE TRADE WAS TRICKS

Georgian folktale as told by
George and Helen Papashvily

T here was, there was, and yet there was not, there was once a king who, like all kings, wanted to believe he was the trickiest man in the whole world.

During the day when his court stood near to applaud each word he spoke, he felt sure of this. But at night when sleep was slow he worried.

Is it possible, is it really possible, he would think to himself, that there might be someone who is trickier than I?

Finally he could endure it no longer, and he called his viziers together.

"Go," he commanded them, "and find the trickiest man in my kingdom and bring him here before me. I will match myself against him. If he loses he must be my slave for life."

The viziers set out and in their travels they met many clever men—such clever men, in fact, that they refused to go back and match themselves against the king for no better reward than a promise they might be slaves.

The viziers grew desperate.

At last one night they came through a fertile valley bordered with thick forests into the street of a poor village. Now this village, you should know, was not poor because it was a lazy village or a stupid village. It was poor because the king owned the valley and all the forest beyond. Each year he took such a heavy rent that no matter how hard the villagers worked when harvest time came, nothing was left for them but the middlings of their own wheat and a few crooked tree stumps.

But poor as this village was, they knew how to act like rich men. They called the viziers to the best supper they could cook and afterward, for their entertainment, built a campfire and told stories.

As the evening sharpened itself to a point, the viziers noticed that one man, Shahkro, was better than all the rest at guessing riddles and remembering poems and describing his adventures.

"Let us see if he will go with us and match himself against the king," whispered the viziers to each other.

At first when they asked Shahkro he refused, but finally after some persuasion he said, "I will go with you, but I will go just like this. Without my hat and without my *cherkasska*."

And exactly that way they brought him before the king.

"Sit down," the king said. "So you think you are the trickiest man in my kingdom?"

"Tricking is my trade," Shahkro answered.

"Try to trick me then," the king commanded. "But I warn you," he added, "it cannot be done for I am so tricky myself."

"I can see that," Shahkro said. "I wish I had known all this before. I would have come prepared. As it was, I left in such a

118

hurry I didn't stop for my hat or my *cherkasska*, to say nothing of my tools."

"What tools?"

"Why, the tools I use for tricking people."

"Go and get them."

"That's not so easy. Naturally, as I'm sure you know from your own experience, I can't just bundle them together as though they were something ordinary. I need wagons."

"Wagons?" said the king. "How many wagons?"

"About a hundred with a hundred horses to pull them."

"Take them from my stable but come right back."

"Certainly," Shahkro said. "With luck I should have everything loaded in five or six months."

"Five or six months?"

"I'll need to bring *all* my tools if I must trick you."

"Well, come back as soon as you can."

"By the way," Shahkro said when the wagons were brought and he was ready to drive off, "if I can't trick you I know I must be your slave for the rest of my life, but just suppose I win, what then?"

"But you can't win," the king told him.

"I know I can't, but suppose I did."

"Well, what do you want?"

"Something you wouldn't miss if you gave it to me."

"I agree," said the king.

Shahkro went home at a fast trot, called all the villagers together,

gave them each a horse and wagon, and
working side by side they sowed and harvested
a crop large enough to last them for ten years.

"At least we have this much out of it,"
Shahkro said, when the last load of grain came
creaking into the barn. "Now bring me all the
empty wineskins you can find."

When these were collected, Shahkro blew
them full of air and piled them on the wagons
and rode back to the palace.

The king was waiting impatiently for him
in the great hall, surrounded by all his nobles
dressed in their richest costumes.

"Let us begin," the king said.

"I must unpack my tools," Shahkro told him.

"I will send servants to do that," the king said.

While they were waiting the king's dog ran
into the room and, noticing a stranger was
there, he came over and sniffed Shahkro's legs
to make his acquaintance.

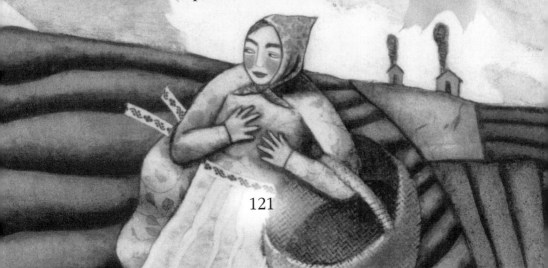

Shahkro bent his head and blew very lightly in the dog's ear. The dog, of course, in turn licked Shahkro's ear.

"This is awful news!" Shahkro jumped up from his chair. "Awful! Where's my hat? Where's my coat? I beg you loan me the fastest horse in your own stable. My dear wife whom I left well and happy yesterday, is dying."

"How do you know?" cried the king.

"How does he know?" cried the court.

"Your dog, as you saw, whispered it in my ear just now."

Everyone was sorry and the king ordered the best horse in his stable saddled, a full-blooded black Arabian, and Shahkro rode away home.

He stayed there long enough to sell the horse for a good price and buy a black donkey. Then he put the horse's saddle and bridle on the donkey and went back to town.

The king was waiting in the courtyard, and when he saw Shahkro jogging along he cried out, "Where is my horse?"

"Horse?" Shahkro said. "Horse! Oh King, have your joke at my expense. I am only a poor man. But I never thought you would do a thing like this to me. Send me home to my sick wife on a horse that changes himself back and forth to a donkey as it suits his pleasure."

"That's impossible," the king said. "I've had that horse for five years."

"Impossible or not," Shahkro answered, "here I am the same as I started out for home five days ago. Here is the same bridle in my hands. Here is the same black animal under me. And it's a donkey."

The king looked at the saddle and at the bridle. He ran his hand over the donkey's flank. "Well, all I can say in apology is that he never did it while I rode him. But let's forget all that. When are you going to try to trick me?"

"Right now," Shahkro said. "Sit down. Answer me a question. You claimed you were a trickster. Did you ever use any tools?"

"No."

"Then why did you think I would? So there I
tricked you once. In all the years you had your
dog, did he ever talk to you?"

"No."

"Then why did you think he would talk to me?
I tricked you twice. In all the years you had your
black horse, did he ever turn into a donkey for
you?"

"No."

"Then why should he for me? There I tricked
you three times. Now pay me and I will go."

The king saw he had one last chance to
redeem his reputation as a trickster so he said,
"Remember, for your reward I promised only what
I wouldn't miss. You must choose something I
never use or otherwise I would miss it. Now what
shall it be?"

"Your head," Shahkro answered.

When the king heard this he began to shake
and turn so green that Shahkro took pity on him.
"Wait," he said, "I will take another reward. Because
on second thought you do use your head. It keeps
your hat from lying on your shoulders. Give me
instead your forest and all the fields around it for
my village people to use for their own."

"Certainly," said the king, and he called his viziers and sealed the agreement right there and gave it to Shahkro. "And now I don't want to keep you for I know you are anxious to get home."

Shahkro went back to his village and in honor he lived there all his life.

As for the king, after that he didn't have to worry anymore whether or not he was the trickiest man in the world, so I suppose he slept very well. Or maybe because he was a king he found a new worry to keep him awake.

"The Emperor is in his dressing room right now."

THE EMPEROR'S NEW CLOTHES

Hans Christian Andersen

Many years ago there lived an Emperor who cared so much about beautiful new clothes that he spent all his money on dressing stylishly. He took no interest at all in his soldiers, nor did he care to attend the theater or go out for a drive, unless of course it gave him a chance to show off his new clothes. He had a different outfit for every hour of the day and, just as you usually say that kings are sitting in council, it was always said of him: "The Emperor is in his dressing room right now."

In the big city where the Emperor lived,
there were many distractions. Strangers
came and went all the time, and one day
two swindlers appeared. They claimed to be
weavers and said that they knew how to weave
the loveliest cloth you could imagine. Not
only were the colors and designs they created

unusually beautiful,
but the clothes made
from their fabrics also
had the amazing ability
of becoming invisible
to those who were unfit
for their posts or just
hopelessly stupid.

"Those must be lovely clothes!"
thought the Emperor. "If I wore
something like that, I could tell which
men in my kingdom were unfit for
their posts, and I would also be able to
tell the smart ones from the stupid ones.
Yes, I must have some of that fabric woven for
me at once." And he paid the swindlers a large
sum of money so that they could get started
at once.

The swindlers assembled a couple of looms
and pretended to be working, but there was
nothing at all on their looms. Straightaway they
demanded the finest silk and the purest gold
thread, which they promptly stowed away in
their own bags. Then they worked far into the
night on their empty looms.

"Well, now, I wonder how the weavers
are getting on with their work," the Emperor
thought. But he was beginning to feel some
anxiety about the fact that anyone who was
stupid or unfit for his post would not be able
to see what was being woven. Not that he had
any fears about himself—he felt quite confident
on that score—but all the same it might be
better to send someone else out first, to see
how things were progressing. Everyone in

town had heard about the cloth's mysterious power, and they were all eager to discover the incompetence or stupidity of their neighbors.

"I will send my honest old minister to the weavers," the Emperor thought. "He's the best person to inspect the cloth, for he has plenty of good sense, and no one is better qualified for his post than he is."

So off went the good-natured old minister to the workshop where the two swindlers were laboring with all their might at the empty looms. "God save us!" thought the minister, and his eyes nearly popped out of his head. "Why, I can't see a thing!" But he was careful not to say that out loud.

The two swindlers invited him to take
a closer look—didn't he find the pattern
beautiful and the colors lovely? They gestured
at the empty frames, but no matter how widely
he opened his eyes, he couldn't see a thing,
for there was nothing there. "Good Lord!" he
thought. "Is it possible that I'm an idiot? I never
once suspected it, and I mustn't let on that it

is a possibility. Can it be that I'm unfit for my post? No, it will never do for me to admit that I can't see the cloth."

"Well, why aren't you saying anything about it?" asked one of the swindlers, who was pretending to be weaving.

"Oh, it's enchanting! Quite exquisite!" the old minister said, peering over his spectacles. "That pattern and those colors! I shall tell the Emperor right away how much I like it."

"Ah, we are so glad that you like it," the weavers replied, and they described the colors and extraordinary patterns in detail. The old minister listened attentively so that he would be able to repeat their description to the Emperor when he returned home—which he duly did.

The swindlers demanded more money, more silk, and more gold thread, which they insisted they needed to keep weaving. They stuffed it all in their own pockets—not a thread was put on the loom—while they went on weaving at the empty frames as before.

After a while, the Emperor sent a second respected official to see how the weaving was progressing and to find out when the cloth would be ready. What had happened to the first minister also happened to him. He looked as hard as he could, but since there was nothing there but an empty loom, he couldn't see a thing.

"There, isn't this a beautiful piece of cloth!" the swindlers declared, as they described the lovely design that didn't exist at all.

"I'm not stupid," thought the man. "This can only mean that I'm not fit for my position. That would be ridiculous, so I'd better not let on." And so he praised the cloth he could not see and declared that he was delighted with its beautiful hues and lovely patterns. "Yes, it's quite exquisite," he said to the Emperor.

The splendid fabric soon became the talk of the town.

And now the Emperor wanted to see the cloth for himself while it was still on the loom. Accompanied by a select group of people, including the two stately old officials who had already been there, he went to visit the crafty swindlers, who were weaving for all they were worth without using a bit of yarn or thread.

"Look, isn't it *magnifique?*"
the two venerable officials
exclaimed. "If Your Majesty will but take
a look. What a design! What colors!" And they
pointed at the empty loom, feeling sure that all
the others could see the cloth.

"What on earth!" thought the Emperor. "I
can't see a thing! This is appalling! Am I stupid?
Am I unfit to be Emperor? This is the most
horrible thing I can imagine happening to me!"

"Oh, it's very beautiful!" the Emperor said.
"It has our most gracious approval." And he
gave a satisfied nod as he inspected the empty
loom. He wasn't about to say that he couldn't
see a thing. The courtiers who had come with
him strained their eyes, but they couldn't see
any more than the others. Still, they all said
exactly what the Emperor had said: "Oh, it's
very beautiful!" They advised him to wear his
splendid new clothes for the first time in the
grand parade that was about to take place.

"It's *magnifique!*" "Exquisite!"
"Superb!"—that's what you
heard over and over again.
Everyone was really pleased
with the weaving. The
Emperor knighted each
of the two swindlers and
gave them medals to wear
in their buttonholes,
along with the title
Imperial Weaver.

On the eve of the
parade, the rogues sat up
all night with more than
sixteen candles burning. Everyone could see
how busy they were finishing the Emperor's
new clothes. They pretended to remove the
cloth from the loom; they cut the air with big
scissors; and they sewed with needles that had
no thread. Then at last they announced: "There!
The Emperor's clothes are ready at last!"

The Emperor, with his most distinguished
courtiers, went in person to the weavers,
who each stretched out an arm as if holding
something up and said: "Just look at these

trousers! Here is the jacket! This is the cloak."
And so on. "They are all as light as spiderwebs.
You can hardly tell you are wearing anything—
that's the virtue of this delicate cloth."

"Yes, indeed," the courtiers declared. But
they were unable to see a thing, for there was
absolutely nothing there.

"Now, would it please His Imperial Majesty
to remove his clothes?" asked the swindlers.
"Then we can fit you with the new ones, over
there in front of the long mirror."

And so the Emperor took off the clothes
he was wearing, and the swindlers pretended
to hand him each of the new garments they
claimed to have made, and they held him at
the waist as if they were attaching something
. . . it was his train. And the Emperor twisted
and turned in front of the mirror.

"Goodness! How splendid His Majesty looks
in the new clothes. What a perfect fit!" they all
exclaimed. "What patterns! What colors! What
priceless attire!"

The master of ceremonies came in with an
announcement. "The canopy for the parade is
ready and waiting for Your Majesty."

"I am quite ready," said the Emperor. "The clothes suit me well, don't they!" And he turned around one last time in front of the mirror, trying to look as if he were examining his fine new clothing.

The chamberlains who were supposed to carry the train groped around on the floor as if they were picking it up. As they walked,

they held out their hands, not daring to let on that they couldn't see anything.

The Emperor marched in the parade under the lovely canopy, and everyone in the streets and at the windows said: "Goodness! The Emperor's new clothes are the finest he has ever worn. What a lovely train on his coat! What a perfect fit!" People were not willing to let on that there was nothing at all to see,

because that would have meant they were either unfit for their posts or very stupid. Never had the Emperor's clothes made such a great impression.

"But he isn't wearing anything at all!" a little child declared.

"Goodness gracious! Did you hear the voice of that innocent child!" cried the father. And the child's remark was whispered from one person to the next.

"Yes, he isn't wearing anything at all!" the crowd shouted at last. And the Emperor cringed, for he was beginning to suspect that everyone was right. But then he realized: "I must go through with it now, parade and all." And he drew himself up even more proudly than before, while his chamberlains walked behind him carrying the train that was not there at all.

141

A Guide to Question Types

Below are different types of questions you might ask while reading. Notice that it isn't always important (or even possible) to answer all questions right away. The questions below are about "White Wave" (pp. 15–23).

Factual questions are about the story and have one correct answer that you can find by looking back at the story.

> **What does Kuo Ming do for a living?** (Answer: He is a farmer.)
>
> **Why does White Wave leave Kuo Ming?** (Answer: She leaves because Kuo Ming forgets he must not try to touch her.)

Vocabulary questions are about words or phrases in the story. They can be answered with the glossary (pp. 147–169), a dictionary, or *context clues*—parts of the story near the word that give hints about its meaning.

> **What does "flourished" mean?**
>
> **What is "earthenware"?** (Practice finding context clues on page 16 to figure out the meaning of this word.)

Background questions are often about a story's location, time period, or culture. You can answer them with information from a source like the Internet or an encyclopedia.

> **Are there a lot of shrines in China?**
>
> **How big are moon snails?**

Speculative questions ask about events or details that are not covered in the story. You must guess at or invent your answers.

> Does anyone else get to see White Wave?
>
> How did Kuo Ming meet his wife?

Evaluative questions ask for your personal opinion about something in the story, like whether a character does the right thing. These questions have more than one good answer. Support for these answers comes from your beliefs and experiences as well as the story.

> Was it right for White Wave to leave Kuo Ming?
>
> Would you have built a shrine for White Wave?

Interpretive questions ask about the deep meaning of the story and are the focus of a Shared Inquiry discussion. They have more than one good answer. Support for these answers comes only from evidence in the story.

> Why does White Wave give Kuo Ming her shell even though he tried to touch her?
>
> Why does Kuo Ming tell his wife and children the story of White Wave?

SHARED INQUIRY
BEYOND THE CLASSROOM

The skills you have practiced in Junior Great Books will help you in school, but they will also help you in other parts of your life. In this Junior Great Books program, you've learned to:

Ask questions. To learn almost anything, you need to ask questions. If you want to know how to program a computer, play chess, or bake a cake, questions can help you understand what to do and why.

Think deeply and search for meaning. By discussing stories, you've learned that you can understand more by going deeper. Lots of things in life are like this, such as movies, art, and the natural world. Spending time looking closely at things and wondering about them helps you understand more about the world around you.

Back up your ideas with evidence. Being able to share your ideas and back them up with evidence are important skills. When you write a paragraph or essay, give a speech, or even ask for more allowance, you need to be able to say clearly what your idea is and why you think it makes sense.

Listen and respond to others' ideas. Even if your first idea about a story is a good one, listening to other people's ideas can help you better understand what you think. You may find new ways to back up your idea, or you may change your mind. This will help you with many things in life, from deciding what sports team to join to who to vote for in an election.

Respect other people's points of view. In Junior Great Books, you've seen that two people can read the same story and have different ideas about it without one person having to be wrong. You have also learned to agree and disagree with others politely. These skills will help you get along with others in all parts of your life.

GLOSSARY

In this glossary, you'll find definitions for words that you may not know but are in the stories you've read. You'll find the meaning of each word as it is used in the story. The word may have other meanings as well, which you can find in a dictionary if you're interested. If you don't find a word here that you are wondering about, go to your dictionary for help.

acclaimed: You **acclaim** something when you give it excited praise or support. *The crowd **acclaimed** the championship baseball team.*

accomplishment: An **accomplishment** is something that has been done successfully and completely. *Beautifully playing a difficult piece of music on the piano is an **accomplishment**.*

admit: When you **admit** something, you tell the truth about it. *The thief had to **admit** he stole the wallet when it was discovered in his bag.*

aimlessly: If you do something **aimlessly,** you do it without a plan or purpose. *The speaker talked so **aimlessly** that everyone got bored.*

anxiety: When you feel **anxiety**, you are very nervous or worried about what might happen. *My friend was filled with **anxiety** when his dog was lost.*

anxious: If you are **anxious** to do something, you want to do it very much and want to be sure nothing goes wrong. *I left the house early because I was **anxious** to get to the movie on time.* **Anxious** can also mean being worried about something. *I had a hard time sleeping because I was **anxious** about the speech I had to give the next day.*

appalling: Terrible or shocking. *You might not be allowed to see some movies because your parents think the violence in them is **appalling**.*

approval: To give your **approval** to something means that you officially agree with it or that you have a good opinion of it. *You might need your parents' **approval** before you go to a sleepover at a friend's house. The dog won first place at the dog show because it had the **approval** of all the judges.*

astonishment: You feel **astonishment** when you are very surprised about something. *You might look at your sister in **astonishment** if she offered to do all your chores.*

attempt: To try to do something. *My mother would usually not **attempt** to climb a tree, but when our cat got stuck in one we were surprised by how high she climbed.*

148

attire: Clothing.

au revoir: French for "goodbye."

bade: Said. **Bade** is the past tense of *bid*.

balconies: A **balcony** is a platform that sticks out from the outside wall of a building, often with railings around it for safety. *Houses and apartments sometimes have **balconies** where people can sit and enjoy the fresh air.*

barge: A long, large boat with a flat bottom used to carry goods on rivers and canals.

basking: To **bask** is to sit or lie in a pleasant warmth or light. *On a cold night of a camping trip, you might spend time **basking** by the fire.*

bawling: To **bawl** is to cry loudly. *The baby started **bawling** when his mother took away the toy he was playing with.*

bellowed: To **bellow** is to make a loud, deep roar. *I **bellowed** at my sister when she broke my bicycle.*

bemused: Someone who is **bemused** is puzzled or confused about something. *The movie was supposed to be scary, but it was so hard to understand that we were **bemused** by it instead.*

bewildered: A person who is **bewildered** feels confused and lost. *There were so many hallways in the building that I got **bewildered** trying to find the exit.*

billowed, billowing: To **billow** is to rise up and move in large waves. *Smoke **billowed** from the burning factory.*

bleak: A place that is **bleak** is bare and gloomy. *We shivered when we went into the empty, **bleak** house.* Something may also be described as **bleak** if it does not have much hope of turning out well. *When it started to rain, we knew that our chances of going to the carnival were **bleak**.*

bobbin: A spool that holds thread or yarn for weaving or sewing.

budge: To **budge** is to move something just a little. *The movers struggled to **budge** the heavy sofa.*

buffalo chips: Dried buffalo droppings.

bundle: When you **bundle** things, you gather them together like a package. *My father asked me to **bundle** the laundry and put it in the car.*

bustling: Something that is **bustling** is busy and loud. *The cafeteria was **bustling** as the cooks served food to lots of noisy students.*

calligraphy: Beautiful handwritten lettering that is often done with a special brush or pen.

calling: Your **calling** is the work you feel you are meant to do in life. *I am good at math, but writing poetry is my true **calling**.*

cantered: When a horse **canters**, it moves at a medium-fast speed. *The pony walked, then trotted, then **cantered** around the field.*

capable: If you are **capable**, you are able to do many things well. *We were not sure he could bake a cake, weed the garden, and fix the car, but it turned out that he was quite **capable**.*

cascaded: To **cascade** is to fall or flow in a way that looks like a waterfall. *The beads from the broken necklace **cascaded** to the floor.*

castanets: Small shell-shaped musical instruments, usually made of wood, that you wear on your fingers and click together.

cataract: A very large, steep waterfall.

chamberlains: The people in charge of the household of a royal person.

chancellor: A type of important official in a government.

charity: Money or help given freely to those who need it. *He showed his **charity** by working at the local food pantry.*

cherkasska: A long overcoat.

claimed: When you **claim** something, you say it is true but can't prove it (at least at that moment). *My classmate **claimed** he could surf, but since we didn't live near the ocean, I never saw him do it.*

clan: A group or family that someone belongs to.

clasped: You **clasp** something when you hold it firmly and tightly. *The woman **clasped** her purse tightly against her chest for fear of losing it.*

clenched: To be **clenched** is to be squeezed together or brought tightly together. *During the roller coaster ride I was so scared I **clenched** my teeth.*

clutched: When you **clutch** something, you hold onto it tightly. *I kept my dog's leash **clutched** in my hand so he wouldn't run away.*

coaxed: To **coax** is to get someone to do something by speaking or acting friendly and gentle. *I **coaxed** my little brother into helping me clean my room by being very nice to him.*

collided: When people or things **collide**, they bump or crash into each other. *The two cars were dented badly when they **collided**.*

concealed: To **conceal** is to hide something. *The student **concealed** his snack so that the teacher couldn't see it.*

conceited: You are **conceited** if you are too proud of yourself and the things you can do. *After my cousin was on television, he grew **conceited** and told everyone he was a star.*

console: To comfort or cheer up a person. *Your mother might try to **console** you if you were sick and had to miss the class field trip.*

content: If you feel **content**, you are happy with what you have and are not wishing for anything else. *My sister wanted to eat the whole pie, but I was **content** with one piece.*

council: A group of people brought together to help solve problems, give advice, or make laws. *The king asked his **council** of wise men and women to help him decide the laws of the kingdom.*

courage: Someone who has **courage** is able to bravely face danger or difficulty. *Firefighters must have great **courage** to go into burning buildings to save people. You would show **courage** if you gave a speech in public even though you were nervous.*

court: The king or queen's royal family, personal servants, and advisers. *The king ordered all the people in his **court** to come to the royal ball.*

courtier: A person who spends time with and helps a royal person. *A **courtier** might wait on a king or queen by laying out clothes or bringing meals.*

crafty: Good at tricking people. *The **crafty** shopkeeper was good at getting people to spend more than they meant to.*

cringed: To **cringe** is to pull away from something because of a feeling of fear, embarrassment, or dislike. *The puppy **cringed** when it heard the thunder and lightning. You might **cringe** if someone was pointing and laughing at you.*

cubit: A **cubit** is a measure of length that is about seventeen to twenty-two inches. Three **cubits** is equal to about five feet. *In ancient times, a **cubit** was measured from the elbow to the tip of the middle finger.*

dacha: A Russian cottage or country house.

debt: If you have a **debt**, you owe something to someone, usually money. *Our neighbor paid the debt he owed us before he left town.*

demanded: To **demand** is to order something to be done or to ask for something firmly. *My father demanded that we stop playing in the mud and clean ourselves off at once.*

dense: Something **dense** is made up of things that are crowded thickly together. *The weeds in the garden were so dense that it took hours to pull them all out.*

desire: A strong feeling of wanting something. *My brother had such a desire for his favorite flavor of ice cream that he went to three stores to find it.*

desperate: You are **desperate** when you feel hopeless about something, or when you feel you need to do something very badly. *You might feel desperate if you had only a few minutes left to answer several questions on an important test.*

devour: To **devour** is to eat fast, taking big bites. *If you hadn't eaten all day, you might devour your lunch as soon as you got it.*

dishonorable: A **dishonorable** word or action brings shame on someone. *The thief was shamed when people found out about his dishonorable deeds.*

distaffs: A **distaff** is a stick that holds wool ready to be pulled off little by little to make into yarn or thread. *Distaffs are often attached to spinning wheels.*

distinguished: People who are **distinguished** are respected or famous because of their talents or skills. *The **distinguished** author has won many awards for her wonderful books.*

drowsed: To **drowse** is to be half asleep or to sleep on and off. *The cat **drowsed** on the windowsill until a loud noise woke him up.*

duly: To do something **duly** means to do it at the proper time or in the correct way. *When the teacher told us it was time for reading, we **duly** took out our books. My father **duly** paid the check after we finished our dinner at the restaurant.*

eager: Someone who is **eager** is very interested in and excited about something. *You might be **eager** to go to a concert put on by your favorite singer.*

earthenware: A type of clay pottery.

endure: When you **endure** something, you put up with it even if it is unpleasant or painful. *You might have to **endure** very cold temperatures when you walk to school in the winter.*

estate: An large area of land with a big house on it.

exquisite: Something **exquisite** is very beautiful or very finely made. *A pink and orange sunset over the ocean is* **exquisite**. *The* **exquisite** *pattern on her coat was made by hand.*

extraordinary: Very unusual or amazing. *The student showed* **extraordinary** *knowledge during the spelling bee, getting every word right.*

famine: A great lack of food. *During a* **famine**, *people may starve because they don't have enough to eat.*

fatigued: Very tired. *After the long hike, the campers were* **fatigued** *and wanted to rest.*

fertile: Easily able to grow large crops.

festooned: Something that is **festooned** is decorated with ribbons, streamers, or other kinds of trim. *For my friend's birthday, the dining room was* **festooned** *with balloons and banners.*

flinch: To **flinch** is to make a sudden, quick movement because something hurts or is frightening. *I tried not to* **flinch** *when the nurse removed the splinter from my finger.*

flourished: To **flourish** is to grow in a healthy, strong way. *The plants* **flourished** *once we put them near a sunny window and gave them lots of water.*

fond: If you are **fond** of something, you have a great liking for it. *I am so **fond** of riding my bicycle that I try to do it even in bad weather.*

fowler: A person who hunts or traps wild birds.

fretted: To **fret** is to behave in a worried or nervous way. *I lost my keys at school and **fretted** all night about whether I would be able to find them in the morning.*

gestured: To **gesture** is to make movements with your body or head to point something out or to show your thoughts or feelings. *The crossing guard **gestured** for us to stop by holding out her hand.*

gleaming: To **gleam** is to shine brightly. *I cleaned the silverware until it was **gleaming**.*

glinting: To **glint** is to sparkle with light. *The snow was **glinting** so brightly in the sun that we had trouble seeing.*

Grand Circus des Étoiles: French for "Great Circus of Stars."

gratitude: A feeling of being thankful. *You would feel **gratitude** toward a friend who shared food with you when you forgot your lunch.*

groped: To **grope** is to feel around with your hands for something you cannot see. *I **groped** for the light switch in the dark room.*

handiwork: Your **handiwork** is anything you have made yourself, by hand. *Knitting and making clay pots are two examples of **handiwork**.*

harmony: Friendly agreement. *The two groups at war finally stopped fighting and began to live in **harmony**.*

hauled: To pull or drag something that takes a lot of work to move. *I was very tired after we **hauled** the heavy basket of laundry up the stairs.*

heave: To give something a **heave** is to give it a strong pull or lift. *We watched the construction crew **heave** a huge load of bricks onto the sidewalk.*

hesitation: The act of pausing uncertainly before doing something. *You might show **hesitation** at the end of a high diving board if you were scared to jump.*

hues: Colors. *A rainbow has many **hues**, including red, green, and yellow.*

humble: Something that is **humble** is not big or important. *The rich businesswoman worked her way up from a **humble** job.* A person who is **humble** doesn't brag or think too highly of himself. *The coach stayed **humble** even though his team won the championship.*

impression: An **impression** is a feeling or thought you get about something or someone. *By working hard and being polite to his teachers, the boy made a good **impression** at school. The mean look on the girl's face gave me the **impression** that she didn't like me.*

incompetence: Not having the skills needed to do something well. *The cook who burned all the food was fired for his **incompetence**.*

inspect: To **inspect** something is to look very closely at it. *I had to **inspect** the sleeve of my sweater to find the tiny hole in it.*

inspire: To **inspire** is to fill someone with a strong (usually positive) feeling, or to make someone want very much to do or make something. *The principal tried to be fair in order to **inspire** everyone to trust him. My father likes to go to parks because beautiful settings **inspire** him to paint.*

intently: When you do something **intently**, you focus on what you are doing and give it your full attention. *The basketball player looked **intently** at the hoop as he prepared to shoot the ball.*

keen: Very sharp. *In the Middle Ages it was important for a knight to have a **keen** sword for battle.*

kitsune: Japanese for "fox." *In Japanese folktales and myths, a* **kitsune** *is a magical creature that can change itself into a human and often play tricks.*

lair: The place, often hidden, where a wild animal lives. *The bear finally came out of her* **lair** *when the weather became warmer.*

lamentation: Crying and moaning with great sadness.

lariat: A rope with a large loop at one end that is used to catch cattle or horses. *The cowboy threw a* **lariat** *around the horse's neck and led it back to the barn.*

let on: To **let on** means to show or admit that you know something. *My best friend* **let on** *that she was planning a party for me and spoiled the surprise.*

local: Someone or something **local** belongs to or is connected to a specific place. *It seems as if everyone in town is friends with our* **local** *barber.*

longing: To have a **longing** for something is to want or wish for it very much. *If you are very thirsty, you might have a* **longing** *for a big glass of lemonade.*

looms: Frames or machines used to weave thread or yarn into cloth.

lurched: To **lurch** is to move suddenly and jerkily, or to roll suddenly to the side. *We almost fell over when the elevator **lurched** to a stop.*

lush: Thickly covered with plant life. *The **lush** lawn looked like an ocean of green.*

mademoiselle: French for "young woman."

***magnifique*:** French for "magnificent" or "wonderful."

majestic: Something **majestic** is grand and suggests royal power. *We were amazed by the size and colors of the peacock's **majestic** tail.*

manor: A large house in the country and the land around it. *In the Middle Ages, a rich lord often owned a **manor** and had farmers work the land for him.*

manufacture: To **manufacture** something is to make it, usually with a machine. *The factories down the street **manufacture** cars.*

meager: If something is **meager**, there is very little or not enough of it. *We were still hungry after our **meager** meal.*

merchant: A person who buys and sells things for a living. *The jewelry **merchant** downtown sells pretty necklaces.* A **merchant** can also be the owner or manager of a store. *The **merchant** proudly opened her new shop on the first day of the year.*

middlings: When wheat kernels are ground up, the smaller, finer bits of flour are removed, and rougher, larger bits called **middlings** are left over. *Middlings are used mostly as food for animals.*

modesty: Someone who shows **modesty** doesn't brag or think too highly of himself or herself. *When the famous singer spoke to us in a friendly way, we were surprised by her modesty.*

monk: A member of a religious community of men who agree to live by special rules. *When the man became a monk, he promised he would not get married or own any property.*

monsieur: French for "mister."

murmured: To **murmur** is for a person or group of people to make a soft, low, hard-to-hear sound. *When people murmured at the back of the class, our teacher asked them to share what they were saying with everyone else.*

occupation: Your **occupation** is the job you do to earn a living. *His grandmother's occupation was teaching school, but her hobby was gardening.*

overcome: To beat or to get the better of something or someone. *I am trying to overcome my fear of heights.*

perplexed: Puzzled or confused. *After losing the instructions, he was perplexed about how to put together the model airplane.*

162

persuasion: When you try to talk a person into doing or thinking something by giving good reasons, you are using **persuasion**. *You might try **persuasion** to get your sister to clean your room for you.*

pestilence: Deadly sickness or disease.

pitiful: You feel sorry for someone or something that is **pitiful**. *When I heard the puppy's **pitiful** whining, I brought him inside and out of the pouring rain.*

plunged: To **plunge** is to dive into something very fast, without fear or without thinking too much about it. *We **plunged** into the lake, even though we knew how cold it was.*

posts: Jobs.

promptly: When something is done **promptly**, it is done right away or exactly at a certain time. *We went **promptly** to the theater when we found out the movie was starting in fifteen minutes. After the bell rings, every student **promptly** starts the morning work.*

purling: When water **purls**, it flows in small, gentle waves with a soft splashing sound. *The birds like to bathe in the fountain's **purling** water.*

qualified: If you are **qualified** for something, you have the skills or knowledge to do it. *Once I take some first aid classes, I will be **qualified** to be a lifeguard at the pool.*

163

ranged: In this story, to **range** things is to place them in a row or rows. *The chairs were **ranged** evenly around the stage.*

redeem: When you **redeem** something, you save it or make up for it when it seems like you are about to lose it. *If you kept making mistakes in a soccer game, you could **redeem** your standing as a good player by scoring three goals in a row.*

registers: A **register** is a book in which official lists are kept. *Teachers sometimes use **registers** to keep track of how many days each student has been absent from class.*

reluctant: When you are **reluctant** to do something, you don't really want to do it. *We were having such a good time at the party that we were **reluctant** to leave.*

reprimanding: Someone who is **reprimanding** you is speaking to you in an angry way because you did something wrong. *The teacher was **reprimanding** the boy for passing notes in class.*

reputation: Your **reputation** is the way people think about you. *Last year my sister had a **reputation** for goofing off in school, but this year she is working harder. The librarian had a good **reputation** with the students because she was always helpful and kind.*

ridiculous: Very silly or foolish. *She wore a* ***ridiculous*** *hat with plastic fruit and flowers all over it.*

riled: Someone who is **riled** is upset and angry. *The principal was* ***riled*** *when someone pulled the fire alarm.*

rippled: To **ripple** is to move like small waves of water. *When the breeze blew through the window, the curtains* ***rippled.***

rogues: A **rogue** is a person who plays tricks or misbehaves. *A* ***rogue*** *stole my lunch money yesterday. Those two* ***rogues*** *are always throwing snowballs at the school bus.*

sacrilege: Not showing respect for something thought of as holy. *In India, many people feel that eating beef is* ***sacrilege*** *because cows are thought to be holy animals.*

sang [somebody's] praises: When you **sing someone's praises**, you say very good things about that person's qualities or talents. *I felt much better about my new math teacher after my cousin* ***sang her praises***.

satisfactory: Something that is **satisfactory** is good enough but not great. *The student was disappointed that even after studying hard, his grade was only* ***satisfactory***.

scorched: To **scorch** something is to burn its surface. *My father scorched his shirt when he set the hot iron down on it.*

shinnied: To **shinny** is to climb quickly up or down something. *The firefighter shinnied up the ladder in less than a minute.*

shrine: A **shrine** is a place created to honor someone. *People often pray at a shrine, or leave gifts or light candles for the person they are honoring.*

slunk: Moved in a quiet, sneaky way. **Slunk** is the past tense of *slink*. *When my mother asked who had broken the window, my older brother slunk out of the room.*

spirited: Full of energy and excitement. *The class had a spirited talk about where to go for a field trip.*

stately: A **stately** person looks and acts in a grand or royal way. *The king walked in a stately manner with his chest out and his head held high.*

sternly: In a serious, firm, tough way. *The captain sternly ordered the soldiers to march into battle.*

stowed: To **stow** something is to put it away carefully. *When we left the park we stowed our picnic basket and blanket in the trunk of the car.*

surging: Something that is **surging** is moving strongly forward, like a wave. *As soon as the doors opened, the crowd began surging into the theater.*

surly: Someone **surly** is mean and unfriendly. *Our **surly** neighbor yells at anyone who steps on her lawn.*

surveyed: To **survey** something is to look over it carefully. *We **surveyed** the park to find the best place for our picnic.*

swifts: Small dark-colored birds that can fly very quickly because of their long, narrow wings.

swindlers: People who take other people's money or property by tricking them. *The **swindlers** pretended to raise money for the hospital, but they kept it for themselves instead.*

synthetic: Something **synthetic** is made by humans and is not found in nature. *Plastic is an example of a **synthetic** material.*

tarry: To **tarry** is to stay in a certain place for a while. *In the summertime, you might **tarry** outside for a few more minutes before going in for dinner.*

thatch: A roof covering made out of strong plant stalks, like straw, reeds, or palm tree leaves.

thrusting: To **thrust** is to push into or go through something with force. *The chef split the watermelon in half by **thrusting** a knife into it.*

to boot: A phrase that means "as well" or "besides." *We couldn't go to the concert because it was in another town, and we had no money **to boot**.*

train: A long part of a robe or dress that trails behind the person wearing it.

transforming: When you **transform** something, you make a great change to it, or you change it into something else. *The artist was **transforming** the lump of clay into a vase.*

tufts: A **tuft** is a bunch of yarn, grass, hair, or feathers that is tied or grows close together at one end. *Many babies have only little **tufts** of hair on their head when they're born.*

Tzar and Tzarina: Before 1917 the **tzar** was the male ruler of Russia and the **tzarina** was his wife.

venerable: Someone **venerable** is worthy of respect because of his or her age, knowledge, or position in life. *The children asked their **venerable** grandmother to sit at the head of the table.*

victorious: A person or group who is **victorious** has won an important struggle or contest. *When they won the game, the **victorious** team jumped up and down and threw their caps in the air.*

virtue: When you behave with **virtue**, it means you know and do what is right. *When you are honest, kind, or helpful, you are showing **virtue**.*

viziers: In the past, a **vizier** was someone of high rank in the government who gave advice to the ruler. *Several hundred years ago, countries in parts of Asia, Africa, and Europe had **viziers** who helped leaders make decisions.*

wearily: If you do something **wearily**, you do it in a way that shows you are very tired. *After mowing the lawn on a hot day, I climbed the front steps **wearily**.*

weft: The threads that go from side to side in fabric or on a *loom* (a machine used to weave fabric). *To make cloth on a loom, threads are woven through the **weft**.*

whimsical: Playful and funny. *The baby's room was decorated with pictures of **whimsical** clowns.*

writhed: To **writhe** is to twist or wiggle around, often because of pain or worry. *The worm **writhed** on the hook as the fish came toward it.*

ACKNOWLEDGMENTS

All possible care has been taken to trace ownership and secure permission for each selection in this series. The Great Books Foundation wishes to thank the following authors, publishers, and representatives for permission to reproduce copyrighted material:

WHITE WAVE, by Diane Wolkstein. Copyright © 1979 by Diane Wolkstein. Reproduced by permission of Rachel Zucker.

LUBA AND THE WREN, by Patricia Polacco. Copyright © 1999 by Patricia Polacco. Reproduced by permission of Philomel Books, a division of Penguin Group (USA) LLC.

BASHO AND THE RIVER STONES, by Tim Myers, illustrations by Oki Han. Published in the United States by Amazon Publishing, 2013. Reproduced by permission of Amazon Publishing.

The Monster Who Grew Small, from THE SCARLET FISH AND OTHER STORIES, by Joan Grant. Copyright © 1942 by Joan Grant. Reproduced by permission of Joan Grant Estate.

THE BUFFALO STORM, by Katherine Applegate. Text copyright © 2007 by Katherine Applegate. Reproduced by permission of Clarion Books, an imprint of Houghton Mifflin Harcourt Publishing Company.

PIERRE'S DREAM, by Jennifer Armstrong. Text copyright © 1999 by Jennifer M. Armstrong. Reproduced by permission of Writers House, LLC.

The Dream Weaver, from EL JARDÍN DE LAS SIETE PUERTAS, by Concha Castroviejo. Copyright © 1961 by Concha Castroviejo. Reproduced by permission of María Seijo Castroviejo. English translation by Helen Lane. Translation copyright © 2002 by the Great Books Foundation.

The Man Whose Trade Was Tricks, from YES AND NO STORIES: A BOOK OF GEORGIAN FOLKTALES, by George and Helen Papashvily. Copyright © 1946, 1974 by George and Helen Papashvily. Reproduced by permission of HarperCollins Publishers.

The Emperor's New Clothes, from THE ANNOTATED HANS CHRISTIAN ANDERSEN, edited by Maria Tatar, translated by Maria Tatar and Julie K. Allen. Copyright © 2008 by Maria Tatar. Reproduced by permission of W. W. Norton & Company, Inc.

ILLUSTRATION CREDITS

Illustrations for *White Wave* copyright © 2004 by Ron Himler.

Illustrations for *Luba and the Wren* copyright © 1999 by Patricia Polacco. Reproduced by permission of Philomel Books, a division of Penguin Group (USA) LLC.

Illustrations for *Basho and the River Stones* by Oki Han. Published in the United States by Amazon Publishing, 2013. Reproduced by permission of Amazon Publishing.

Illustrations for *The Monster Who Grew Small* copyright © 1992 by Mary Jones.

Illustrations for *The Buffalo Storm* copyright © 2014 by Gordon Morrison.

Illustrations for *Pierre's Dream* copyright © 2014 by Carll Cneut.

Illustrations for *The Dream Weaver* copyright © 2004 by Vladyana Krykorka.

Illustrations for *The Man Whose Trade Was Tricks* copyright © 1992 by Frank Gargiulo.

Illustrations for *The Emperor's New Clothes* copyright © 1992 by Brock Cole.

Cover art copyright © 2013 by Rich Lo.

Design by THINK Book Works.